Stop Discrimination
We, all are human beings, Almighty's blessing arts.

S Afrose

Ukiyoto Publishing

All global publishing rights are held by

Ukiyoto Publishing

Published in 2024

Content Copyright ©S Afrose

ISBN 9789360492540

Edition 1

All rights reserved.

No part of this publication may be reproduced, transmitted, or stored in a retrieval system, in any form by any means, electronic, mechanical, photocopying, recording or otherwise, without the prior permission of the publisher.

The moral rights of the author have been asserted.

This is a work of fiction. Names, characters, businesses, places, events, locales, and incidents are either the products of the author's imagination or used in a fictitious manner. Any resemblance to actual persons, living or dead, or actual events is purely coincidental.

This book is sold subject to the condition that it shall not by way of trade or otherwise, be lent, resold, hired out or otherwise circulated, without the publisher's prior consent, in any form of binding or cover other than that in which it is published.

www.ukiyoto.com

To
The dearest sister
"Shayela Parveen"

May Almighty bless you always

Acknowledgement

Thanks a lot Dear Almighty for blessing me always.

Thank you so much dear parents, friends, readers, well wishers.

My paradise of words, is my dear heart, full of compassions and love.

Onward can't define. So? Let it come with the dreamy waves of poetic arts.

Love for all, from the deepest core of my heart.

From Author Desk
© S Afrose
Dhaka, Bangladesh, 25th jan-24.

Preface

The sound can't tolerate anymore. Hey you, stop right now. Don't dare to be here. Just leave. Ouch!

Why and why?

Give me a reply. I am waiting.

Why don't, I be here?

Why can't, we be here?

What are our faults?

Explain, pls explain.

You are poor, he is black, she is crippled and so so...

OMG!

How silly those thoughts!

Really?

You think so.

The era, full of these nonsense vibes. Ouch!

It's mandatory to recover. Rectify the nonsense shouting. Stop those words.

"Don't discriminate.

Stop discrimination."

As we all are Almighty's blessings arts. You can't deny this fact. Just accept with respect and love.

Then will see the shore of peace on this earth. It's definitely true.

Stop Discrimination... a poetry book, containing many unspoken words of this part. We have to wake up from the nasty zone afterall. It's our duty to be here with all, forgetting any discrimination, to move happily onward.

So cool. Let's enjoy. Care and Love for all.

As for example- **No Discrimination, Voice, Different We're** etc.

Hope you will enjoy this book. Take this one as a part of your favourite heart.

(For any kind of unwanted words, just pardon.)

Thanks!

From Author Desk ♥

©S Afrose, Bangladesh. 25th Jan-24.

Contents

What?	1
No Discrimination	2
Behind The Scene	3
Holding The Love	4
Voice	5
Soul Hunter	6
Different We are	7
Judgemental Mind, Never.	8
Bloody Thoughts	9
Let's Join Hands	10
For What Reason?	11
Is that not erasable?	12
Just Like A Disease	13
Expect Freedom	14
The Cage	15
Hold This Hand	16
You, The Idol, Little Angel.	17
Racism, So Sad.	19
My Wish	21
The Morale	22
Awareness	23

A Wrong Melody	24
Words	25
From Nature	26
Humanity Flower	28
Black Colour Is Our Pride	29
My Voice	31
Social Rift	32
By Birth	34
Poisoning	36
Not Hidden Anymore	38
Chase By Race	40
Cash Out	42
Blue Lake	43
Open The Door	44
Regarding Your Request	45
Recall The Consequence	46
Don't Ask Me Doing This	47
Demon	48
The Stage	49
Biased	50
Really?	52
Another Year	53
Retreat	55

Spark	56
Among Them	58
Words	60
Melody Of Life	61
Backside	62
The Sunflower	64
Face From Past To Present	65
My Song	66
The Flying Bird	67
The Tiger	68
Mind Says- Hi	69
The Board	70
Ringing	71
Faulty Decision	72
Sleepy Sun	73
Sleepy Time	74
Chilled	75
About the Author	77

What?

People, don't come near.
It's the reserved place,
For us.

You are not welcome.

What?

Are you serious?

Do you like?
I don't.

Then?
Fist of heart,
A new art,
Just overall the part.

What???

(10th Jan-24)

No Discrimination

We can't forget our words
Once again, in the graveyard.
Now the sound of heart,
Pls, hold on this part.

Crying!

No reply.
Only tears-
Falling.

Crying birds.
Ah!
Why?

They fly,
The beautiful ride isn't here.
Why?

They are not familiar,
Not get any drop
Of the dearest love.

Oh no!
It's not right,
Crying under the tree.

(11th Jan-24)

Behind The Scene

Background, not clear.

Something is there,
Someone helps.

Who is there?

Behind the scene,
A shabby attire,
A bright attire.

What?
What do you like?
Say and love.

Behind the scene,
You picked
The desired bridge.

Hiding the original motion.
Is that fair?
Not... but the situation is not clear.

(11th Jan-24)

Holding The Love

Will you love me?
As usual,
I love you so much.

Stop.
Forward, not welcome.
You can't love.

You are poor,
You are the dirty beggar.
How can love?

Just the broken brick.
Rubbish, go away.
Never come back.

How can possible?
Poor? My fault?
I can also love.

My heart beats!
My mind also sings,
The song of love.

(11th Jan-24)

Voice

Midst the nature
A flower,
It says- hello.
It scatters ray of heart.

Midst the life
Walking,
Cautiously.
A voice is heard...

Discrimination?
What?
Let's go for the shining attire.
That is waiting for you, all.

Wear,
As a newborn;
Feel and hear-
The Voice of Heart.

(11th Jan-24)

Soul Hunter

A soul hunter
He is,
Comes
To snatch anyone,
Whether Friend or Foe,
Not a matter.

He doesn't care
Anything.
He doesn't like
Any excuse.
When it is the time,
He comes
To take with him.

Without any discrimination,
He loves the panel at last,

For maintaining the world's equation.

(11th Jan-24)

Different We are

Accept this part.
Access the universal heart.
Did you give that chance,
To show the universe?

We are different
Nothing else to say.
As, different we are,
With vibrant views and arts.

You have too much
You have not,
So what, this option?
Simply similar.

As we are
Differently beautiful.
So love this matter,
From the deepest heart.

(11th Jan-24)

Judgemental Mind, Never.

Be careful.
Be the beautiful pool.
Judge, for what?
Any sign of the birth?

Judgemental mind, never.
She or he, so what?
Different ethnic, Different ways.
Different shades, Different rays.

People's Parliament!
All are similar,
Not same like you or I,
As we are differently adorable ones.

Respect each other.
Access the cutest heart.
Accept this part,
This is picturesque my sweet earth.

(11th Jan-24)

Bloody Thoughts

What's wrong-
Dear earth, dear heart?

Forget?
What's that?

Acting as a demeanor.
Why?

The colour of blood
Is red.
Can't you see?
All hearts beating as usual.
What do you feel?

Your bloody thoughts,
Corruption of mind,
Discrimination rises;
Not right.

All are human beings.
No separated song , no more rings.
See and capture,
Not this bloody hunter.

(12th Jan-24)

Let's Join Hands

Listening, so good.
So cool..
So?

Go ahead.
Spread forward, this message.
We do.

We didn't,
But now-
We have to do.

What?
Let's join hands.
Make the distorted free lane.

(12th Jan-24)

For What Reason?

Think twice
Before saying these same words.
You can't,
You haven't.
You did?
Just go to hell.

Surprised!
For what reason?
We judge someone,
Without any concrete source.
Not fair.
We have no right to conclude this art.

We can't utter those words.

As we know,
Almighty didn't make,
Then-
For what reason, we will?

(12th Jan-24)

Is That Not Erasable?

How does it come?
When earth smiles
Upon some of them.,
Rusting badges flash.

Is that not erasable?
You hope not,
I hope so.
Then, why, the silence?

Mark your words,
Towards the world.
Literally all are gems,
Accept and spread the purest essence.

(12th Jan-24)

Just Like A Disease

Discuss this fact-
'Discriminate'

However,
No single space,
How can get the pace?

Just like a disease,
It spreads.
Two sections always exist on the lively earth's stage.

Rich or poor,
Black or white,
Whatever...

Treat,
As the disease;
Mark this state.

We must eradicate this disease forever.

(12th Jan-24)

Expect Freedom

People, we are here.
We want only
Your care and love.
Just as dear ones,
Dear Friends.

We don't want
To be your slavery army.

Free us.
We expect freedom.
It's picturesque,
Beyond the shadow
A new expectation.

Pls accept us.
Free us.

We expect freedom from all the heinous norms.

(12th Jan-24)

The Cage

Break the cage
Which held you,
As a slave.

Break the cage
Which held you,
As the broken shell.

Break the cage.
Your mind can fly,
Not be a caged bird, forever.

Fly and cry, for what?
Only for the happy life.
Obliged.

(12th Jan-24)

Hold This Hand

The trip
Of the nature.
The life!

I am not used to.
No matter,
You can learn.

I will help,
Just believe.
Just believe.

Hold this hand.
How amazing!
The trip on the earth.

When people say-
We are similar,
We love to stay with all.

Don't forget this overall.

(12th Jan-24)

You, The Idol, Little Angel.

A little child, she is.
Playing-

Galaxy's heart.
Sparkling-

Heaven seeks something very special.

A dreamy palace
Rolling.
Rock and roll-
Hearing.

Two eyes,
Peeping always.

A door opens.
Uncontrolled wave.
For what?

Mind soaks.
Where?

You're idol,
Little Angel.

The earth!
Losing spirits,

Stop Discrimination

Demons are everywhere.
Why and why?

Ouch! A graveyard!

Lack of consciousness.
Lack of empathy.
Ouch!
Ouch!

Lack of faith.
Why and why?

Need to pray for the beautiful earth.
Little angel inspires all the hearts.

We must protect little angels.
We must nourish that paradise.
We should need to follow that way,
Which shows the ray of love.

Holding hands of love,
Forgetting the discrimination parts.

No war can take place ever,
Make this earth, the supreme beautiful hub.

(12th Jan-24)

Racism, So Sad.

The aura of heart
Always shows,
Way of the beautiful life.

Become the owner of this part,
It helps you to feel,
How marvellous!

Racism!
So sad.
My name is not bad.
But the bad taste of the words…

Halt!
Don't make the bridge
To separate,
All hearts.

Different shades,
Different costumes,
Different cultures.
So?

Similar simply.
But not same,
Still; all are human races.
Yes, trace the pace.

Over all the adversity,
Make this in reality.
Hold on the stage.
Humanity and Humanity!

(12th Jan-24)

My Wish

Making wish-My wish!

A wish for the future earth.
A sweet essence!
From the hub of heart.

Making wish-My wish!

A wish for spiritual power.

Slavery, the mid-point of universe.

The power will beat any danger.
The danger that will be died forever.

Making wish-My wish!

A wish for dear ones.
They will stay with us.

Let me make a wish.
An earth with equality sense,

Crown of love,
It can conquer all the parts.
Every part has its own beauty all over.

(12th Jan-24)

The Morale

Being a human,
Being a part of the earth,
Desperately we want,
We will be the blooming flowers.

The morale
For all
The same tune,
Always sing the song of love.

The love
For all,
No discrimination,
Make the cosmic waterfall.

Watching,
Listening,
Accepted?
Expecting…

(12th Jan-24)

Awareness

It's the duty
For all,
Making the society
Dreamy pool.

He or she,
Who are you?
Who I am?
The parts of this society.

Treat this way,
No segmented ray
Of failure or winner;
We all are trying the best, dear.

Away from
All the nasty prospects,
Make the fragrance through-
Your tunnel of Awareness.

(12th Jan-24)

A Wrong Melody

Nobody!
I see.
Anybody?
Let's see.

A wrong melody,
Holding the knob
Of mind.
Shoot!

Shoot right now,
Make it easy.
Repair,
The customer is here.

Who are they?
Your dear ones.
My dear ones?
Everybody!

Make it this time,
Right tract, right tune.
For tracking,
The long journey of life.

(12th Jan-24)

Words

Care your words
When trying to use,
It may damage any heart.
It may kill anyone.
You have no idea.
Peculiar?
Never.

It's true
Realized.
Reality on the road,
Your every word
Turns to be the sword.
To kill any heart.
Collapsed, forever.

It's tricky.
Picking.
Picky
Sticky.
Fridge
Your words,
When they work as lovers;
Only by showing some respect and love.

(12th Jan-24)

From Nature

Never mind,
When you will get the code
From the nature.

Nature is the best,
Making the sense
Of unique essence.

Nature makes the crest
For us,
For making the supreme pace.

No race.
Biased?
Never.
Everyone is most welcome here.

No hidden scar,
No hidden love,
No hidden war.
Nature is equal for all of us.

Rich or Poor
Black or White
Tall or Short
Man or Woman...

How many times
You may define?
No segregated points
The unique potion, for all.

From nature,
Social contract
Should be clear.
This is equality for us.

(12th Jan-24)

Humanity Flower

Make it clear
See the layer,
Desired peer
Humanity Flower.

Be first to set
To make any stage,
To be the pioneer
Garland of Humanity Flower.

Always this part
Not so tough,
Really wishing dear
Humanity Flower.

Make the garden
Take care,
Your heart and mind
Also with this ward.

Humanity over humanity
Making the serenity,
Without any fear
Take this Humanity Flower.

(12th Jan-24)

Black Colour Is Our Pride

We are not worthless,
We are not scapegoats,
We are nothing but human beings.
You have to realize.

Black colour is our pride.
We are not sinners.
Boldly mobility, not allowed.
Can you say, why and why?

We are black.
You are white.
Anything, wrong?
We can't define.

We are not sinners.
We are not your slaves.
We are not born to abuse.
We are here with humble choices.

Black is better than your words.
Black is better than any site.
The night is covered by darkness,
Nobody can deny to see this natural art.

Darkness has its own beauty.
You may be forgotten, we don't.
We are black blessed,
We are as like as yours'.

Stop Discrimination

Don't mock us as dirty bards.
Don't chock our thoughts of hearts.
Don't put your legs on our heads.
We are not demons-aliens.

(12th Jan-24)

My Voice

Something happens.
My voice stucked.
My legs stopped.
I am the fallen shell.

From where to where?
Who will care?
My voice!
Anybody hears?

No sound.
On or off,
The same tune.

Ah!

Only,
Echoing
My voice.
Strange!

(12th Jan-24)

Social Rift

Any gist?
You have the gut
To say,
You are right.
You will not give up.

Great.
It's necessary
Always.

Society has lost,
The essence
Of moral standards.

Making,
So many
Social rifts.

Let's make up
Those unwanted parts.
Unity is the universal.

Social rift?
Just bullshit.
We will not allow this.
Is that right?
Care and share.

(12th Jan-24)

By Birth

By birth,
You are there
And I am here.

So?
No excuse.
No expectations?

Why?
You hate.
You know the choices.

I don't.
Why?
Who creates this objective?

Details.
Give me the letter.
The link,
I will try.

Is that my own choice?
Where I will be born?
Strange!

Are you sick?
Are you out of mind?
Pls say and say.

It's not fair.
Place of birth!
How does matter?

We are unique,
Source of light.
The universal life!

That's the matter
Don't make this so fussy.

Feel this part

You will know the meaning of life.

(12th Jan-24)

Poisoning

Poisoning, the society.
By growing,
The factory of
Discrimination.

Poisoning, the soul
Of earth,
Which amuses with love.

Devils or not,
Good or not,
Prospective, different.

Rectify by the deeds,
Not by human being itself.

A baby comes on earth
With the golden heart.
The seed of Poisoning darts,
Force to make
The poisonous viper.

Probably it's still,
Not so late,
Just come on
And take the step.

We must nourish this part
Humanity is the supreme pace of the dearest earth.

(12th Jan-24)

Not Hidden Anymore

Dawn starts.
Another chance
Another say,
Just go away.

Oh!
It's enough.
Now
We will not hide.

Not hidden anymore.
What will you do?
Try.
We will not cry.

We prefer our lives,
Not for your holistic vibes.
Joyous parts?
Damn care!

Did you hear?
Voice of a stranger-
Voice of a strong mother-
Who will welcome her?

You never…
Very funny.
Heart cries.
How peculiar this earth!

Go to hell
You bloody shells,
Don't shed tears
We will make the fire.

Then fine
By this time,
We will say
Not hidden anymore.

(12th Jan-24)

Chase By Race

Not acceptable.
Not anything.
Nobody can do this time.
Whole in the dream,
Midst the earth.

Chase by race.
Can trace,
Who is the best?
Me or not.

Who will judge?
You or we?
Who will see?
Who doesn't?

Chase by race.
Access or accept?
Show me some details.
Defeated Fascist.

Shut up!
Dear heart.
Don't utter
Or will start the bloody fight.

Chase by race
Not your choice.
It contains
The seed of grace.

From the previous verses
The project of earth,
Probably pride of the pristine world,
Now not qualify.

(12th Jan-24)

Cash Out

Go out
Or
Cash out.

Box out
Or
Shoe out.

Cash out
Or
Cash back.

Cash out
Perhaps perfect.

(13th Jan-24)

Blue Lake

Full of tears
There,
The base.

Place of dream,
Place of life.
Blue Lake.

Literally love
No fight back
You may guess.

Is it that?
The dreamy shade,
Blue Lake!

(13th Jan-24)

Open The Door

Break the rule and
Open the door.

No excuses.
We will be fused.

Confused!
Where is the knob of the door?

Shut up!
Shut up!

Relax
And search the knob.

Open the door
Not appropriate for the fast move.

(13th Jan-24)

Regarding Your Request

Here I am
With you,
Regarding your request.
Host, am I?
Fine.
Not right?
Oh!
I see.
You have made this choice.

Where I am?
Nobody
Or anybody?
Unwanted fear.
But why?
You don't know.
I also don't know.
Then,
Where is the soothing rain?

(13th Jan-24)

Recall The Consequence

Not allowed.
Then, what can be in the contract?
Any clue?

Recall the consequence.
Received your request.

What is there?
The website of mind.
Anything else?
I have no sense.

Recall the consequence.
And then get the pace.

(13th Jan-24)

Don't Ask Me Doing This

This is the last time.
Don't ask me doing this
As usual.

This is my choice.
I am not used to,
I don't like.

Pls let me explain.
Let me express myself.
Can't?

Don't ask me doing this again,
As per your choice.
I am not your slave.

So respectfully,
I say this again,
Don't make this tough time for all of us.

(14th Jan-24)

Demon

You are not familiar.
Human?
Never.

You look like a demon.
The demonic mart!
Demon, you're.

Always shouting,
Don't like anyone.
Clear.

Make your turn,
Make your thoughts,
You are always the reflection of Demon.

(14th Jan-24)

The Stage

Upside
You are right,
The stage
So tough.

Upside
I am not,
But my words
Always the blocks.

To be or not,
Help me.
I am here,
Your favourite ladder.

Come on and check.
Cheer-
Go Upside,
Ladder of tears, stopped.

(14th Jan-24)

Biased

Those two minds.
Conditional,
Conflict.

Biased!
Oh! I see.
Always you have seen.

Biased
For this time,
No dear.
Let me speak.

It's for you
It's for me
It's for us
It's for the universe.

Twisted for a while,
Now it's time.
Just hold
And ready.

Blast
The past,
Flashback
The heart.

Biased
Something,
Someone,
Now collapsed.

(14th Jan-24)

Really?

Again the chance,
Don't be surprised
When you see,
The wave of blood
From dearest heart.
Really?
I love to see.

Share and dare
With your dearest part
Of the life.
Of course dearself
Without any fear.
Really?
Love to hear again.

Drops of blood
Squeezes always.
Whatever,
Anything, Anytime-
Again the, flashback of heart.
Really?
Love to see & hear.

(14th Jan-24)

Another Year

Existing year
Walking gradually,
Making satisfactory territory,
Hopefully some clichés are unique sources.
Need to revive, taking the precious zone.

Don't worry my dear.
You can hear the echoes of earth.
The time tunnel is there,
Another year is waiting here.
Yes! It's another year.

Let's go and watch,
Where is the legend of heart?
It's in the deepest port,
You have to realize.
Wow!

Another year is already here.
Ready to make the ride of life.
Again with your pride and pride.
Phonetic vibes...Wow!
How wonderful!

So pretty so precious,
Hopefully a gorgeous tower.
Will be ahead, my dear.
You will be the emperor.
Your favourite temple of life.

It's your time,
Need to shine.
Making the galactic rhyme.
At each nook, the sunshine.
What a beautiful sight!

(14th Jan-24)

Retreat

Lastly, seen
Now, been
A new scene.

Retreat.
It's the proper time
Just read and comment.

Retreat.
Dear mind
Soul in disarray.

Windows closed.
Oh no!
Sure about that.

Survey.
Thank you!
Then make the choice.

Retreat!
Again
The real life's street.

(14th Jan-24)

Spark

Those are there
So silly
So shabby.
No one has asked.
No preference.

Then,
A sound.
What's that?
A great look,
Spark.
Behind the berg.

Ice-berg!
Life's diverse.
Then a cooler
Making the way,
The warmth touch,
Most welcome.

Spark!
Even
When the world
Is said,
Don't;

Never lose your temple of mind.

Spark,
And then say-
I am here.
Spark,
Is my right.
You can't snatch.
You have no right.

(14th Jan-24)

Among Them

Only one boy
Crippled,
Can't make the way
As per his smile.

Crocodile tears
Here and peer,
Gear on his side.
So pathetic,
Ah!

Among them
He is all alone.
No friends.
Only the emotions dance,
As mocking sense.

He is crying.
Why and why?
What's my fault?
I don't know,
I am here by God's grace.
He has made this platform.

So tough.

Nobody wants to love.

Why? Am I a ghost?

Pls see,

Pls say,

I can also love.

Juts feel and make the prospective views.

(14th Jan-24)

Words

More or less, it's fine.
When words come as sunshine.
Making heart a cosy set
Mind stucks in the same stage.

Take care of your each word.
It can break any heart or earth.
Also the magic of words,
Can make a beautiful lane or paradise.

Words make the sense of friendship,
Words make the clan of foes.
That's the power of words.
We have to accept and realize.

Words say always
We love and enjoy this place,
Pls don't destroy the beautiful universe,
We will be your dearest peers.

(14th Jan-24)

Melody Of Life

Once upon a time
The guitar,
Lays with my mind.
Making so many notes,
With lovely rhythms.
Melody of life!

Today
The same guitar,
Lays with my mind.
Making no effort,
To be the best song,
At last.
Why and why?

Melody of life!
Lost.
Melody of life!
Must be restored.

If not
Then life can be collapsed,
At any time
Melody of life , Ah!

(14th Jan-24)

Backside

Garden of dreams
Garden of reels.

Garden of dreams
Garden of fears.

Backside
The paradise.

Can't make
The trip on the stage.

What's the matter?
Make the plan.

Backside
Full of pains.

Lost the way to track
Nobody wants to set up this one.

Ah!
Backside!

The round shape
The sun is there.

It tries
To shine the upstairs.

Now ready
And then make the desired panel.

Backside
Fuel of your life.

(14th Jan-24)

The Sunflower

A dream!
Sweet fragrance,
Sweet dream.

The sunflower!
The shadow of mine.

Once was
The smiley hub,
Sweet happiness.

The sunflower!
Ready dear.
This is my dream.

The sunflower!
Helps to smile,
At any state of the life.

(14th Jan-24)

Face From Past To Present

Never forget,
Facing
From past to present,
Your existence.

Twisted
Mused,
May be,
But-
Awesome yourself.

Face the past.
Any dust?
Just clean,
And judge yourself.

Face the present
The trailer the train.
You have to be strong,
You have been there.

Just make this always.
Forget once
But not always,
Face the each and every segment.

(14th Jan-24)

My Song

I will sing this time
I will make my rhyme.
You can hear or not
That's your problem, not mine.

My song!
My song!
I sing the song.

My song!
My song!
My dear sweet mall.

I will do this time.
I will show this time.
No rifts can be here,
Discrimination… A shameless matter.

Every time is fine,
Everyone can see,
The reflection of the mind.
My song is my life!

(14th Jan-24)

The Flying Bird

Make this part.
Without any art
The process
And the passion…

The junction!
Blurred, once.
For what's reason?
Take this caption.

A call!
No more hesitations,
Give me supreme power dear Lord,
I will make the precise conclusion.

(25th Jan-24)

The Tiger

When the form
Comes
From your inner part,
The tiger;
Your hidden power
Rising up.

You know
I know
No more rifts,
An art
No distracted part
A paper of the white mind.

The tiger
When comes,
Starting the fight.
Naturally we see
It's fine,
The tiger is your valid sign.

(25th Jan-24)

Mind Says- Hi

Hi dear all,
Hope you, fine.
Never mind,
Mind says bye.
Oh no!
Sorry.
Again, it says- Hi.

What's up?
Catch the part at each social rite.
How sweet!
A cute kite on the azure's hub.
I know this site.

Little to elder ones,
Without any fear
You can see,
You can say;
I am fine.
As the sweet pie,
Mind says, Hi!

(25th Jan-24)

The Board

Reconsider
Technology,
Reconsider
Your thoughts.

The board of life!
You know
I know,
Without any rustic vibe.

Lost project
Lost the word.
Not be here
Clearly known by the fair side.

The board
The bosom of mind,
How sweet!
I love this time.

(25th Jan-24)

Ringing

Don't hear?
How comes?

Don't listen?
Not right.

It's the issue
You have seen.

Same azure
Same zephyr.

Always here or there
Everywhere.

No discrimination
No distracted mind.

So nice
Free of mind.

Ringing…
Alert the world.

(25th Jan-24)

Faulty Decision

Literally
Make this caption,
Your faulty decision
Corrupting the proper position.

A fresh start!
Faulty decision?
No more captions,
Take the precautions.

No idea,
You have taken this.
You have to know,
Your favourite motion.

(25th Jan-24)

Sleepy Sun

Cringe Crinkle,
Minutes mingled.
Life ouch!
Sleep comes.
No time
For singing,
Oh no!
Sleepy sun!

How does it act?
No ray.
Who says?
I am fine.
Thanks or not,
Crazy mind!
Sleepy Sun!

(25th Jan-24)

Sleepy Time

The clock is dead
The clock is set.
A sign of mind!
Sleepy time.

Sleepy Sleepy!
Nice to fit,
Fit to sit,
Get the suitable part.

Sleepy time
Saying,
Goodbye!
We are fine.

(25th Jan-24)

Chilled

Seat!
Chilled there.
Sitting rather than fitting
A new ray catching.

Chilled!
Filled, desired potential vault.
Words of mind-
Saying,
We don't like to be dumb.

(25th Jan-24)

"THANK YOU SO MUCH
FOR YOUR LOVE,
TOWARDS MY TINY CANVAS,
STOP DISCRIMINATION
RIGHT NOW"
© S AFROSE, BD.
25th Jan-24

About the Author

S Afrose

Author S Afrose (Sabiha Afrose, from Bangladesh) has made her writing realm since August- 2020. She enjoys each of the part of this writing ward. She tries to express the hidden word or emotion, by her words; with the glamour of poetry. Poetry is her best friend. Her writes have been published on magazines and anthologies (90+) . In this writing realm, she has achieved many awards beyond her expectations (eg. Doctorate in Literature from Instituto Cultural Colombiano, Literoma Laureate Winner 2022, Mahatma Gandhi Award 2023 from Instituto Cultural Colombiano, One of the World Record Holders for Hyperpoem, etc.)

Published author of poetry books- **Thanks Dear God, Poetic Essence , Reflection of Mind , Glittering Hopes, Angels Smile, Tiny Garden of Words, Dancing Alphabet, Artistic Muse,**

Essence of love, The Magical Quill, Dear Children, Haunted Site. Woman, The Butterfly, A Little Fantasy, Lion's Roar, The Bride, No War, Friendship, Happy Christmas, A New Beginning, Bluish Ocean, A Bouquet of Love.

All are available worldwide (on Amazon.com & from publication hub and from other sites also as any format). Apart these, there are some

Bengali and English poetry books (available on rokomari.com in Bangladesh).

Her mother is Selina Begum and father is Manirul Islam.

Educational achievements- B Pharm, M Pharm from Jahangirnagar University, BD.

Favourite hobbies are reading, writing, specially the poetry section.

Contact-

afrosewritings@outlook.com

sabiha_pharma@yahoo.com

You Tube: S Afrose *Muse of Writes*(@safrose_poetic_arts)

Facebook page: Muse of Words by S Afrose

Twitter:@afrose2020

Inst. @safrosepoetryworld

"STOP DISCRIMINATION"
A NEW CAPTION
MAKE THE MOTION
WITH LOVELY ACTION
© S AFROSE, BD.

www.ingramcontent.com/pod-product-compliance
Lightning Source LLC
LaVergne TN
LVHW041624070526
838199LV00052B/3236